For Jasper – J.W.

For Max McGinty – A.R.

Also by Jeanne Willis and Adrian Reynolds:

THAT'S NOT FUNNY!

American edition published in 2011 by Andersen Press USA, an imprint of Andersen Press Ltd.
www.andersenpressusa.com

First published in Great Britain in 2011 by Andersen Press Ltd., 20 Vauxhall Bridge Road, London SW1V 2SA.
Published in Australia by Random House Australia Pty., Level 3, 100 Pacific Highway, North Sydney, NSW 2060.

Text copyright © Jeanne Willis, 2011. Illustration copyright © Adrian Reynolds, 2011

Distributed in the United States and Canada by
Lerner Publishing Group, Inc.
241 First Avenue North
Minneapolis, MN 55401 U.S.A.
www.lernerbooks.com

Library of Congress Cataloging-in-Publication Data Available.
ISBN: 978-0-7613-8093-1

Color separated in Switzerland by Photolitho AG, Zürich. Printed and bound in Singapore.

1 - TWP - 3/7/11

I'M SURE I SAW A
DINOSAUR

**Jeanne
Willis**

**Adrian
Reynolds**

ANDERSEN PRESS USA

One foggy, groggy morning
by the salty, splashy sea . . .

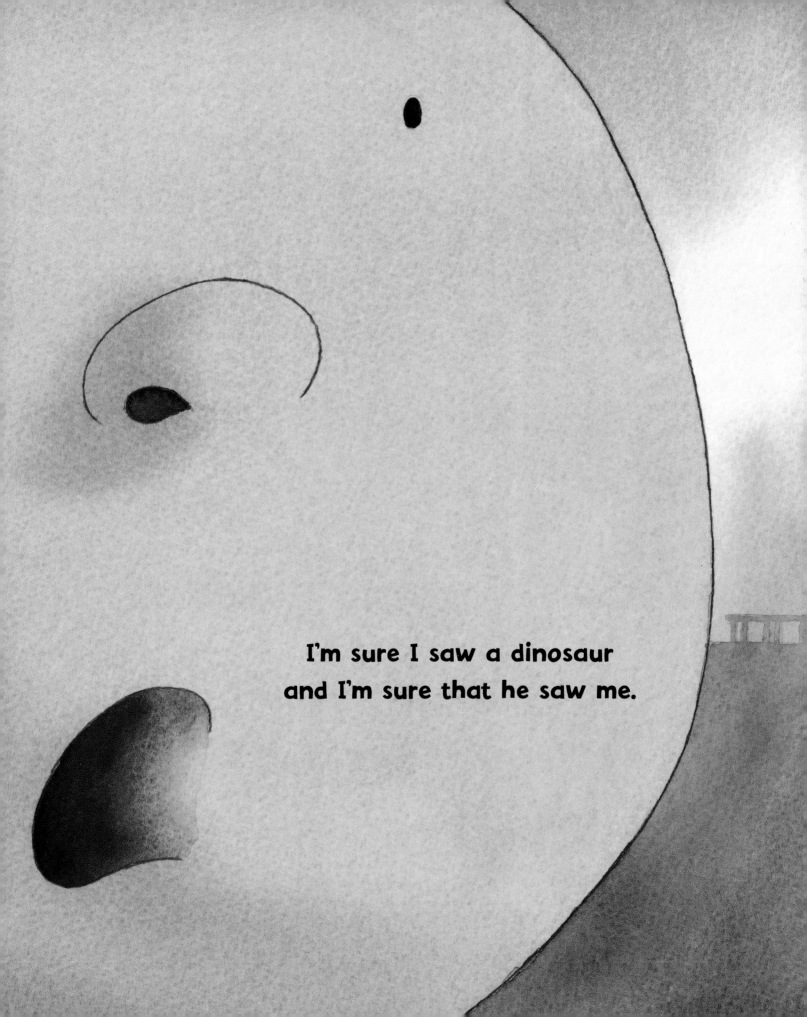

I'm sure I saw a dinosaur
and I'm sure that he saw me.

I ran and told the fisherman,

who ran and told his mum,

who ran and told the butcher
he must hurry up and come.

The butcher told the baker,
and the baker told the vet,
and they ran down to
the seashore
with a camera and a net.

"What's the matter?"
asked the priest.
"Now what is all the fuss?"
"A dinosaur's been seen!"
they said.
"We're sure it can see us!"

The priest told all the people,
and each person told a friend.
They all came running down the beach
to Sandy Bottom End.

All the aunts and uncles came,
the nephews and the nieces.
All the grans and grandads came
in woolly hats and fleeces.

They came with sweets and sandwiches
and soup inside a flask.
Some didn't know why they were there
but didn't want to ask.

The newsmen came, the navy came.
The captain called his crew.
"A dinosaur's been seen!" he said.
"Make sure it can't see you!"

They came with ropes and motorboats,
with cannons and with snares.
They came with swords and submarines
and scientists and prayers.

The air force came. The army came
and formed a human chain.
Men in parachutes arrived
and jumped out of a plane.

They came with dogs and divers
and binoculars and bait
and searched the sea for dinosaurs
from morning until late.

They sat out in the wind and snow.
They sat out in the rain,
and none of them showed any sign
of going home again.

They set up camp upon the sand
in tents and trucks and cars,
and still they sit and watch and wait
beneath the moon and stars.

But will they see a dinosaur?
Or was my master plan . . .
to help my daddy sell ice cream?
He is the ice-cream man!

No one comes to buy them
in the winter when it's cold.
Now everybody wants one.
Every frozen treat's been sold.

I'm sure I saw a dinosaur,
but is it really true?
Come and buy an ice cream . . .

. . . and perhaps you'll see one too!